Derek Owusu is a writer, poet and podcaster from north London. He discovered his passion for literature at the age of twenty-three while studying Exercise Science at university. Unable to afford a change of degree, he began reading voraciously and sneaking into English Literature lectures at the University of Manchester. Derek edited and contributed to *Safe: On Black British Men Reclaiming Space*. *That Reminds Me*, his first solo work, won the Desmond Elliott Prize in 2020.

Also by Derek Owusu

Safe: On Black British Men Reclaiming Space

That Reminds Me

About This Boy: Growing Up, Making Mistakes and Becoming Me (with Leon Rolle)

Losing the Plot

Borderline Fiction

HUNGER PAINS

Derek Owusu

For Melissa, my friend always

Part 1

Chapter 1

Okay, so basically this all started at my boy's party. One thing I remember thinking was *why the fuck am I chewing so fast*, because I wasn't even hungry. The chicken was dry, and as I bit down through one piece and hit my tongue bar the pain shot through my gums to my jaw and then down my spine all the way to my stomach. I moved my tongue around inside my mouth, and touched the sharp pieces of a broken tooth. *Fuck sake*, I thought. Sobering stuff.

I walked upstairs to the bathroom. Once I was inside I spat into the toilet, blood and everything, and touched down on the broken tooth. I was pissed, but I won't lie, there was a tiny bit of relief there because it was a back tooth that no one would notice, but still. I unscrewed the piercing, dropped it in the toilet, ran the tap and washed out my mouth. I was looking to grab some mouthwash I could see under the sink, but true say when people swig that stuff, food and shit from the same day or day before drop back into the bottle. Nasty.

Water was calm, was fine, and after a few minutes sitting on the closed toilet seat, I was feeling better. I was ready to go back into the party.

Every year, Jeremy throws a party, and every year, I hook up with a different girl. The mandem like to call me a gyalist, galdem sugar, ladies' man, gyaldem glucose and all the rest, but it's never really been like that for me. Basically I don't really go out, more time you'll just catch me at work or in the gym. And moving to girls in the gym isn't even worth it. Always turns out to be stress. So whenever I decide to actually leave my yard, I try to have a good time, you get me. And girls are a good time, even without sex, I just prefer being around them.

But at the party, after I'd broken my tooth, I wasn't really feeling it. I kept sliding my tongue through the new gap in my teeth and could taste the blood. Imagine lipsing someone and they taste that? So yeah, obviously wasn't looking to move up gyal. Was tryna focus on myself as well, anyway. And it's annoying because only reason I was eating that chicken was because I wanted to semi-enjoy the last day of my old diet and training. After that, focus only. I knew exactly what I wanted to look like and I knew I had the genes and willpower to do it. Just about timing, patience and planning. And women can be a distraction. Nah, actually, that sounds bad. Not really a distraction, but more time you gotta give them attention you could be putting somewhere else, get me. And I wasn't trying to do that right now. So yeah, I was thinking no distractions. Or only a few minor ones.

Anyway, there were loads of tings at Jeremy's. And everyone looked good. Even the mandem looked decent. I walked back into the party, back into the room with all the food, and gave the chicken on the table a dirty look before finding my seat again. Couple of us man were sitting in a corner just chatting nonsense because the other room, where everyone was dancing, was rampacked. The door was closed but it sounded like all that shouting and off-key singing was mixing to form one giant voice whose bass was trying to break through the wall. If you put your hand flat on it, you could feel it.

'Yo, Ray, where you been?' said Jeremy.

'Ran toilet real quick,' I said.

'Toilet, yeah? Who you up in there with? Couple man saying they saw you take one ting with you?'

'Who said that?'

'Streets is talking.'

'You're annoying. Where's everyone else gone?'

'To enjoy the dance. Mandem can't draw gyal as quickly as you. Not everyone banging gym every day.'

'Yeah, yeah,' I said.

I was about to leave, folded myself backwards to crack my lower back, bare stiff and sore from doing deadlifts the day before. I probably could have lifted more but I didn't wanna to push it, get me. 180kg on deadlift is calm. Next would be 190 and then 200. That's where I would stop, though, no interest in going further than that. I ain't a powerlifter. Anyway, my new diet and training plan would have kicked in by then. I actually couldn't wait. Gonna change the fitness game. But yeah, back at the party my back didn't crack but it still felt good. One wave of dizziness hit me straight after and it was one of them where I wasn't sure what caused it. Or maybe I was. Sometimes I swear I ignore myself.

'Go flex in the other room, man,' said Jeremy.

'Don't be a hater?' I said.

'Party in the next room. Unless you wanna be chilling in here on your ones tryna show people you go gym.'

'Nah, I'm going. Just wanna chill for a bit.'

'How much you pushing now, anyway?'

'On what?' I said.

'*On what?* You know.'

'More than last time we went. Up to 172lb now. But that's gonna change soon.'

'On what, though?'

'Nah, I mean that's how much I weigh now. Well, how much I weighed this morning.'

'You weigh yourself every morning?'

'Tracking my progress, innit.'

'For this dangerous new plan you been chatting about?'

'It's not dangerous, man, just . . . fearless?'

'Aight Mark Henry,' he said. 'If you say so.'

'Mark Henry? What the fuck. How am I like Mark Henry?' I said.

'Huh? I'm talking about the wrestler.'

'I know, but how is that me?'

'Reh, calm down, man. I'm saying, weren't he like world's strongest man or something? Why you switching for?'

'Oh.'

'Ray, man, what are you on?'

'Nah, nothing. I thought you were trying to say man's fat.'

'And you were coming to fight man because of that?'

'Nah, sorry.'

'Aight. I'm out. Go catch a whine instead of stressing out weight.'

As Jeremy walked out the door, someone else walked in. I remember thinking straight away, *where do I know this girl from?* The room I was chilling in was basically where all the food was. She walked past me to where the table was and I turned my head, following just a little piece so it wasn't obvious I was looking.

From my corner, I watched the side of the girl as she was picking bits of food up and putting them on her paper plate. She was wearing some red linen dress, and from my angle her bum looked like she banged gym as well, but true say those dresses can lie to you sometimes. Her arms weren't ripped, though. Instead, they were smooth but you could still see those lines where her shoulder cut above the long bicep head. Anyway, this was me thinking she went gym in the first place. I looked at what was on her plate and it was bare protein. Fried chicken wings, some curry goat, mac and cheese, ribs, spicy beef chunks on those kebab sticks. Either she hadn't eaten all day or she was trying to sober up. I don't know how long she'd been at the party but it was kinda late to be eating like that. Even still, in that moment I just wanted to see what her mouth tasted like with that mix up in there even if that meant she had to taste the blood from mine. It was my indulging day, anyway, so it would be calm. I think this was the start of my stomach pains as well. Because I swear I wanted to put my hand into my belly and pull out whatever was moving mad in there. I was so deep into these thoughts I didn't even clock her walk up next to me.

'Hi, Ray!' she said, still picking at the things on her plate.

'Oh, hi, you alright,' I replied, turning fully now.

'Yeah, I'm fine. Why are you in here watching people eat?' she said.

'Nah, I was just chilling for a hot sec. The other room is too hot.'

'I haven't seen you in there.'

'Yeah, I was only in there for a bit.'

'You don't remember me, do you?'

'Of course I do.'

'From where?'

'I'm saying, I remember you but not from where, if you get me?'

'So what's my name then?'

'Rah, why you questioning me like this?'

'It's Temi.'

'Okay? Temi. Now what?'

'Don't be rude.'

'I'm just playing. You know I'm playing.'

'I'm going now,' she said.

'Yeah, safe.' *Safe* you know. I don't even know why I said that. I swear down, sometimes I don't know what I'm thinking when it comes to gyal.

Chapter 2

I opened the door to the living room, basically the dance floor, and walked in half skanking to Crazy Cousinz' 'Do You Mind', dropping low once I crossed the threshold. I gave the DJ couple gun fingers because it was actually a vibe. Most people were two-stepping but their arms were doing a lot more, in the air, out wide, by their sides but with energy. There were people leaning up against the walls but their heads were bopping to the point you knew they were about to join the centre. I carried on dancing and was looking around for that girl. I swear, I had no idea who she was but obviously we must have met somewhere and spoke. I was two-stepping now as well, crossing one hand back and forth across my chest, looking at the floor mostly but still looking now and then for this girl.

When she finally caught my eye, she was sitting down in a corner, drinking something. Her plate was by her foot and there was no food left on it. Just bones and sticks. I was a bit baffled because she wasn't wearing red anymore. Her summer dress was mainly purple. She saw me looking and smiled but I looked away because ain't no way I was trying to look thirsty. Just carried on with my little dance, my head down, preeing the wooden floor. I won't lie, I knew she was gonna either walk up to me or start dancing close but I had to style it out. Had to act like I hadn't noticed her. Honestly, I smelled her before I saw her. She smelled like one perfume I've sometimes clocked on the London Underground in the morning on the way to work. I never know where it's coming from but I try to follow it. Either me and this person who wears it get the same route every morning at the same time, or bare people wear it. It smells like fruits and I'm always hungry after. Anyway, this girl, she was basically dancing in front of me at this point. And when I looked up, she was just there staring, moving her weight from one foot to the other, not even two-stepping. Bruh, I'm not joking, she was just staring like she didn't care. My stomach was hurting again and I swear I couldn't hear the music anymore. I was looking back, though, like, *yeah, okay, now what?* I wasn't going to move to her in this packed room listening to Funky House, c'mon now. So we just danced together where we were, not touching or anything but just at the right distance where you know you're locked onto each other. I swear, it was so intense that I think other man were probably thinking she was my girl, or something. Anyway, we'd been doing this for three or four songs now when she grabbed my hand and pulled me over to the corner where she'd been sitting. I sat down and she sat on my lap. I was tapping my foot and she was rolling her bum cheeks back and forth on my leg. I know you know what I was thinking, that if I get hard right now it's gonna be long, maybe even on a sexual harassment ting. So I had to focus, and started thinking about gym, just to make sure my semi didn't start rising and pressing up on her thigh. It was already a bit awkward and I knew she'd get up and walk away thinking I was too horny. So to try and keep things calm, to take me out of the moment, I started picturing my gym and my session from the day before. About how even though I hit my personal best on deadlift, I failed on my dumbbell press.

Chapter 3

I trained at one of those LA gyms, not too expensive but not cheap either. When you walked into the reception area and had to get your card scanned, all you could smell was chlorine – even though the pool was on the other side of the building. The receptionists were nice and polite and handed you a towel as soon as you walked through the barrier. I won't lie; I had moved to a couple of them before and maybe that's why more time they were nice. Because I'd seen members whose card had flashed red, insufficient funds or whatever, and they'd be quick to turn on you. This happened to me once, but I managed to finesse it and ended up on a date with the receptionist who helped me buy some time for my direct debit. I used to keep bare shit in my locker, all my food and protein. I would get so stressed if I hadn't had my shake at least twenty minutes after my workout. Some of the personal trainers told me that don't matter but I was still shook about it. Like I'd wasted my session if I didn't have 40g of protein in time.

The gym floor had everything you needed, really, loads of squat racks, pull-up bars, dumbbells that went up to 50kg. And thankfully weight plates with a hole in the top so they were easier to carry about. They had straps for every body part too, even your neck, but I'd never seen anyone using that one, still. So yeah, commercial gym stuff but still a bit gritty, if you get me. And of course personal trainers roaming about like they were animals on some grazing ting. Sometimes even posting up behind equipment and watching someone's technique so they could lunge in at the right time. The gym floor didn't smell like chlorine, it actually smelled like blood.

But yeah, whenever I was doing a one-rep max strength day (as much as I can press or pull for one repetition) to check my progress, I always started with deadlifts. Then I'd move onto squats, then pull-ups, then dumbbell chest presses. And you gotta make sure you've had your creatine before, and maybe even an apple for that extra energy. Possibly some nitric oxide if you're on that kinda stuff. But yeah, I was training with my boy Ross. He was one of those 'bro science' guys but he had more knowledge about real science than he did about that anecdotal knowledge that bodybuilders pass down. He was a stiff guy, one of those man where their trap muscles show no matter what they're wearing, and he always had one vein going through his bicep. He looked good, to the point I know most people wanted to look like him, except for me, of course. My ideal, and I know people think it's funny, but my ideal is Brad Pitt in *Fight Club*. I just want pure muscle on my body. No fat, no water, just muscle. And if I look small, that's calm, because I know when I look in the mirror I'll be happy with what I'm looking at. I want to be bigger than Brad, obviously, but lean like that at the same time. And I know how to achieve all this. It's all about diet, really, but I'll show you about that later.

Anyway, so deadlift done, squats done, pull-ups done. All personal bests, by the way, and this was supposed to be my last day for all this strength training too, so I was even more gassed. But then comes the dumbbell bench press. I was going with the 50s. I don't want to blame Ross because obviously I was the one lifting the weight. But he didn't understand, like, he didn't get that when I can sense hands under my elbows, it puts me off. It makes my body relax a little bit because it thinks it's safe. So this is what I was feeling when I was trying to get the weight up. I told him to move but he said, 'Don't worry, I gotcha.' Idiot. I didn't say nothing again because even speaking draws energy out of you. I kept pushing, gritting my teeth, my arms wobbling a little, becoming embarrassed. Then I actually felt his hands and that was it, I dropped the weights.

'Ray, mate, you could have got that one,' he complained.

'Nah, man, I told you don't do that. It puts me off,' I said.

'I only touched you when I saw you needed help.'

'Yeah, but that's what I'm saying. You always . . . you know what, forget it, man, it doesn't matter. I wasn't getting it up, anyway. Safe for that.'

'Listen, mate, try some rotator cuff exercises for a few weeks and I bet you get it up after that.'

'Yeah, cool, thanks.'

'You're alright, mate. You read that book yet, by the way?'

'What book?'

'The Neil Strauss one. How many books have I lent you?'

'Too many, to be honest.'

'You're riot, Ray.'

'Anyway, nah, I haven't read it yet. Just trying to focus on planning my programme first.'

'It'll probably help with that as well.'

'I just don't wanna be distracted. I'll get to it.'

'Speaking of a distraction,' Ross went on.

'What?'

'Over there. On your right. Just look over your shoulder. Don't turn all the way around, you bellend.'

'Oh, her. What about her?'

'Well, she's not here to train, is she? Not dressed like that.'

'It is what it is, man.'

'But it's not, though, is it? I bet if I tried to talk to her she'll tell me to do one even though she's asking for it . . .'

'I'm gonna do some intervals.'

'Yeah, alright, I wait for you in the steam room.'

'Alright, in a bit,' I said.

Ross walked off to hit the treadmills and I sat on the bench for a little while just thinking about my failure. It was pissing me off. The girl Ross was chatting shit about walked past me and her bum *was* basically hanging out. Well, half of it was, anyway, but I couldn't see what there was to complain about. It was like the perfect shape. Like a peach you could munch on. *Fuck it*, I thought. I put on my headphones and scrolled to 'Rose Tattoo' by the Dropkick Murphys. I lifted one dumbbell onto my knee, then the other; waited for the chorus in the song and then fell back onto the bench. I breathed out as I was pushing up, my elbows shaking but stable. And then they were up. No time to celebrate because I thought I had one more in me, the last bit of energy that would no doubt leave me tired the rest of the day. I lowered the dumbbells slowly, taking in a deep breath, and then out and I pushed up again, inch by inch, making sure not to lock out my arms at the top. Boom. Done. I brought the dumbbells down gently and then dropped them either side of me.

I sat up and looked around the gym to see if anyone clocked me. No one, but I bet they were looking when I was lifting. It felt so good I swear I wanted to walk up to that girl, the sexy one, and slap her bum. Nah, actually, I'm chatting shit. I wanted to grab her. Nah, not grab her, hold her from behind, hugging her basically, and lift her off the floor like one excited yout with his girlfriend. Obviously I didn't, but shit, man, she was nice. I felt too good, like, nothing compares. I was so gassed. I swear I can even feel it whenever I remember it. Maybe Ross being around when I was lifting was making me weaker. He was a shit spot, man. I knew say when I told him he'd think I was lying. Oh well. I put everything back on the racks, tried to find the right numbers, and then walked over to the treadmills.

Chapter 4

So yeah, anyway, back at the party now, and me trying to visualise something else obviously didn't work. I swear, everything always comes back to gyal, it's mad. She stopped moving from side to side and was just still for a hot second and then turned and looked down at my face. If I tried to act like I didn't know what was happening, I could blow the whole ting. I'd be left sitting there like some idiot and she'd just chat to a next man. Or I could lean into it, firm it and act like I wanted her to know wagwan. So in the end I put my hand on her back and applied a bit of pressure to bring her closer to my face. But I probably didn't even need to do all that because as soon as my hand slid up her back, she was already moving toward my face. And then of course we just started lipsing while sitting there. This only went on for about ten seconds because then she got up and took my hand again, pulling me through the room. Everyone was still vibing to Funky and were doing couple synchronised dances, tribal skank and all that kinda thing. So no one really noticed us leave the room and then go upstairs. I don't know how she knew where to go and that no one would be there, but she showed me into an empty room and closed the door. I turned around and that was it, she was all over man. I can't lie, I was going with it and lipsing her up but I was a little bit shook that she was gonna taste blood and think I was nasty or nervous but also because this wasn't even my yard. Listen, I'm on gyal and everything, I don't mind hooking up, but this was moving bare quick, and allow having sex when any minute someone could walk in. I'm not on them tings there. My stomach felt windy, not like gas from food, but like some gust twirling up green leaves inside me. But Temi didn't care. I could taste the spicy beef and jerk chicken in her mouth mixed with Hennessy, which was probably what she was drinking when I preed her. When I sucked one of her lips, though, it tasted sweet, so maybe she was mixing drinks. Maybe it was Baileys, so I thought that must be why she must be moving like this. Don't get it twisted, it's not like I was telling her to stop. Nah, I was feeling her up and doing my ting as well. But then she took off her bra and that's when I had to say something because, bro.

'Yo, what if someone comes in?' I said.
'They won't,' she said.
'Are you sure?'
'Ray, this talking isn't sexy.'
'Alright, alright.'

I ain't gonna describe for you what happened next, but just know we didn't beat that day because I said I wanna see her again so let's wait. I wasn't running game, I was really feeling her, feeling Temi. Her telling me it ain't sexy when I was moving shook was actually sexy to me, like, she knew what she wanted and I loved it. So yeah, anyway, there I was, falling in love with some double D breast in my mouth. Ay, life is mad, you know.

Chapter 5

The next morning, I was hanging. I didn't even drink that much but then I remembered my new diet and I'd only had about 1,500 calories before I reached Jeremy's yard for the party. I climbed out of bed, put my feet on the floor and enjoyed the soreness. Two-stepping really come like taking a long walk sometimes. My head was spinning and I felt like I was going to be sick, but it wasn't an unpleasant feeling. Sometimes, if you get lucky, the way the hangover feels can be euphoric, if you get me. Like, yeah, you still feel the nausea, but there is no anxiety, just this feeling of existing in a world you're actually happy to be part of.

First thing every morning I step on my scale. I have to put it in the same place in the kitchen otherwise the reader gets a bit weird. All over my house the floor is uneven, and the kitchen, with tiles and all the rest, is the only place where it feels level. I didn't expect the numbers to be down because the alcohol makes me hold water. So yeah, I was up. By like 4lbs! Bruh, I nearly dashed the scale into the fridge. That shit drives me fucking nuts. True, I know the reason and it all makes sense but seeing it just pisses me off. Like the scale is trying to mock man or something.

I skipped breakfast and just backed a litre and a half of water through the morning. Then I bought a Lucozade Sport at the off-licence near my yard and also backed that in one long squeeze. Had to get those electrolytes in. In my bag I had some chopped-up pieces of steak for lunch and was gonna get some raspberries from another shop on the walk up to the hotel. I think people thought because I ate a lot of protein, I was fucking up my stomach. But what they didn't see is how much fibre I used to eat. Because I can't lie, bowel cancer had me shook and I'd been seeing so many young men get diagnosed. And I know say diet has a lot to do with it. But you'll never see them chatting nutrition in the mainstream media like other things. I swear down, I'm not even chatting when I say the food they sell is trying to kill us. I wouldn't be surprised if all that ultra-processed shit is manufactured for population control or something. Anyway, man rarely touched that stuff, and when I did it was only because there was nothing else and I was about to get a hunger headache. I was thinking all this on my way to work but in the back of my mind trying to get my attention was Temi. She was so nice, man, so buff, so sweet, like, literally I could still taste her lips. When we'd stopped moving mad in Jeremy's room and started talking, she told me about her life and shit. She told me she was a journalist but mostly wrote obituaries. I'd never heard of anyone doing that before, but I guess there's a load of jobs that we think just randomly get done, but obviously someone is doing it.

'What made you want to start doing that?' I asked her when we'd stopped lipsing and she'd put her breast back in her dress.

'Do you really wanna know or you're just asking because you think you have to?' she said.

'Why would I think I have to?'

'I'm not stupid, Ray, I know you men think asking questions is some cheat code to beat and show you care.'

'Oh, right. No, honestly, I'm interested.'

'Hmmmm. Well, basically one of my family members passed away and I . . .'

'Yeah?'

'I was in so much pain. I can't even describe it verbally. So I started writing about it. About how much I loved them and how much joy they brought me. And I started to feel better. And any time I would feel that surprise of realising they're gone, I'd remember something I wrote about the grief. And it would dull the pain. I published it on my website to announce the death. There were a lot of comments but I didn't read any of them.'

'I hear you. I'm sorry.'

'It's okay. After the funeral, people were coming up to me saying how much they loved my eulogy, which I basically adapted from the obituary.'

'I never even clocked there was a difference, you know.'

'So basically, the obituary is more formal. It's written to be published and give the public or whoever a sense of who the person was. It's mostly factual stuff. Not much emotion, even though mine obviously broke that rule. So you're talking about the life of the person. But a eulogy can be full of emotions – joy, pain, humour, regret, anger, and how it relates to the person you've lost. And it's during the funeral service that it's read by a friend or family member. Realistically, an obituary can be written by anyone. So that's what I do. I do it because I want to help people through that sort of pain. Just knowing there are people experiencing it the way I did makes me want to help.'

'Damn, okay. That's actually cool. Not even gassing, I rate it.'

'I like doing it. I'm hoping I can channel all these feelings into a book one day. A novel.'

'Novel?'

'Like a work of fiction? Yeah, man, I really want to write a novel. I want to write about things and people no one else does. Or no one cares about until they read my book. That's one thing you learn from writing obituaries – people are so much more interesting and have done so much more in life than many of us even care to realise. Do you get it?'

'Yeah, I get you.'

'What do you do, Ray?'

'I work in a hotel.'

'That's cool.'

'It's calm most the time, yeah. Nothing to do with death. Though some of the branches have a problem with people checking in and then hanging themselves in the rooms.'

'You think that's a problem for the branches?'

'Yeah, man, it's stressful. Sometimes the hotel

has to be closed for a few days or a week. And no one gets paid. I've spoken to someone who found a body and she had to be signed off work for eight weeks with only half-pay, can you believe it!'

Chapter 6

I arrived at the hotel, the only job I'd ever had. I looked around the lift as it took me up to reception and clocked things I knew Ruby, the manager, would have clocked too. I didn't like to stress her too tough, so usually when I noticed something, I'd just take care of it without her asking me to do it. But my mind was so gone and all over the place. Actually, all over Temi, and plus the smell of the morning breakfast buffet was making me feel even more sick. So I just ignored it, the dust and smudges on the mirror, but picked up the two Diet Coke cans in the corner. You know when you don't sleep enough, or when you sleep too much, or when you wake during a sleep cycle? Any one of those things and the day feels like you're walking through one layer of dream that followed you into reality. Plus man was hungry and hanging, so everything just felt more intense. Maybe I weren't even in love, I thought, and I was mixed up because of all those things. Anyway, I walked past reception, into Ruby's office, sat down in her spare chair and put my head on her table.

Ruby was sitting next to me sorting out the float for the till. This was supposed to be my job. But she'd done the night shift and had my back about certain things too. I had a lot of time for Ruby. Even though she was my manager, there was never that conflict-of-power thing that happens sometimes. Like, we got on well and I'd even chat to her outside work if I bumped into her. Only weird thing about her was that she said her name when she spoke. I know there's a name for it but none of us at work knew, and we just got used to it, anyway. You know what, I think she might have been translating sentences in her head and it just came out like that. Anyway, when I came in and dropped in the seat, she swung around on her chair, still counting money, and was like:

'Are you in a mood?'

'No,' I said.

'So have you done the room checks?'

'Ruby, you just saw me walk in.'

'Maybe you did it before. How would Ruby know?'

'I haven't. I'm hanging.'

'Now you're drinking?'

'Sometimes.'

'Drink with us then?'

'You know I hate you all. Who am I on shift with?'

'One day Ruby will take you seriously. Check the rota.'

'Can you check it for me? I feel sick and I think I'm in love,' I said, to see her reaction.

'You're on shift with Omar.'

'Okay, that's not so bad. Can you stay till twelve, though?'

'Ruby is tired.'

'So am I. Please. I'll do a night shift at some point.'

'Write it down.'

'What?'

'Write down what you said. You'll do a night shift for Ruby. Sign and put on the wall so Ruby doesn't forget.'

'Yeah, whatever. I will, just let me rest for a minute.'

'The love makes you sick?'

'I didn't this morning. Nah, actually, I did. I did feel sick but not like this. It's the smell from the kitchen.'

'Love heals you. Ruby knows.'

'There is a fine line between love and nausea.'

'From one of your books?'

'James Earl Jones. King Jaffe Joffer. Fine, ergh, let me get up. I'll do the room checks first.'

'Who is this person you're in love with?'

'Temi,' I said, as I lifted my head and squinted my eyes at Ruby.

'Everything is drama. Eat something and feel better.'

'I'll actually be sick.'

'It's up to you. Let Ruby finish checking the till.'

'Ruby, you were the only one on shift.'

'So? Even Ruby makes mistakes.'

I got up, leaned back and tried to crack my back, then stretched my arms and bent forward to steady myself from the light-headedness. I checked the rota, had a look at the checklist of occupied rooms and the cleaning records, and headed to the kitchen. I held my nose as I power-walked through, hating the smell of whatever we cooked, saying 'what's good' to the chef and spudding him with my free hand. Then I took a deep breath and held it as I opened the fridge and put my food containers inside. Some old dusty fridge and I swear someone forgot a hidden carton of milk somewhere inside years ago. Nasty. Then I ran back to reception and breathed out, hard, and I swear I felt a little bit of vomit trying to come up. I remember thinking afterward, it's not even just this hotel food that makes my stomach start moving mad these days. Even when I thought about certain meals outside of that nasty-arse kitchen, I knew my face was screwing up. And then I'd get this disgusting taste in my mouth. All those years of eating ultra-processed foods still tainting my tastebuds. Anyway, after that, I began my checks, starting from the fifth floor and working my way down.

Chapter 7

Everything was fine, really, no one had trashed a room or been smoking inside it and taken the smoke detector to pieces. Sometimes you'd even find vomit in the centre of a room or in the middle of the bed, pieces of undercooked hotel chicken goujons or microwaved pizza bits all up in there. Whoever stayed in those rooms would check out in the morning as well. Imagine. So either they threw up in the morning and thought *fuck it*. Or they did it earlier and just chilled in the room with the smell of stomach acid and food stinking up the room. You'd always know when you were about to open a room like that because the smell was so strong you'd clock it in the corridor. The only issue was there weren't enough cleaners. So usually there was no way they'd be able to clean the amount of rooms they needed to. Like, they wouldn't be able to have them ready for the 2 p.m. check-in.

On this day, the head cleaner, Huda, was still on the fourth floor when she should have been on the third already. I asked her wagwan and she told me, talking bare fast and panicky. I wanted to put my hand on her shoulders and try calm her down, tell her everything will be cool. But I caught myself. Huda was stressing, telling me it wasn't fair and all that. Nothing I could do about it. All of us were understaffed, and that's why Ruby was there doing night shifts while her kids were home alone. District manager didn't care as well. As long as we're hitting targets. I said all this to Huda and then was just like 'lemme help you clean some rooms'. She gave me the list, showed me to the cleaning cupboard, gave me a Hoover and then said thank you. Mind you, this entire process had happened before so I don't know why she thought I didn't know where everything was. So anyway, I did my thing, pulling those sheets tight, wiping those tiny tables, emptying bins, blah blah, you know how it goes. When I got back to reception, Ruby nodded at me while a customer was complaining about the Coke machine. Apparently, only syrup was coming out. That's proper nasty work, man. This is why you'd never catch me drinking or eating anything in that place. Trust me, as soon as you step into the kitchen of a budget hotel, you ain't eating food in any one of them ever again.

'Ruby, I'm done,' I said.

'Were you helping them clean?' she said.

'Why you even asking, you know I did.'

'Look how much you love us.'

'Yeah, whatever.'

'Yes, whatever. Even if you won't come out with us but will drink with other people. Ruby sees you.'

'First of all, you know I don't really drink like that. And secondly, you guys always go out to eat. I don't eat what you guys eat.'

'You can bring your packed lunch; we won't judge you.'

'Ruby, shhh, man,' I said.

'The way you all talk to me.'

'What do you want me to do next?'

'People are starting to come in. Help Omar on reception.'

'Yes ma'am.'

'I told you stop calling me that.'

'It's a sign of respect.'

'So what do you call your mum?'

'Ruby, it's not "mum", man, it's "*ma'am*".'

'Don't call me man, either. Go help Omar and let Ruby get ready for her conference call.'

I stepped out of her office and closed the door. The smell had kinda gone now or I'd already got used to it. The complaining customer had gone and my colleague Omar was just there leaning against the wall with his arms folded. I knew that customer had pissed him off.

'Wagwan, G,' I said.

'Yeah, what's good?' he said.

'Just here, man. What was that customer saying?'

'Nothing important.'

'That why you look stressed?'

'No person can stress me.'

'I met one girl yesterday.'

'She Muslim?'

'Where am I going to meet a Muslim girl, Omar?'

'Not everyone on their Deen. So you could meet them anywhere.'

'Nah, she's not Muslim. Actually, I haven't even asked her. Oh shit, imagine she is and I was sucking her breast . . .'

'Don't talk like that about sisters!'

'Yeah, nah, for real, my bad.'

'So you're in love?'

'I actually think I am, you know.'

And from then I just started chatting bare, telling him shit I know he didn't really care for, but when you're at work, pretending to be interested passes the time more quickly. There wasn't even a lot but I stretched it out, because I wanted to say out loud how I was feeling, like, just to make sure it was real or whatever. I told him about Temi's small eyes. Her big appetite. Her weird job. Her compassion. Alla dat. He was just stood there listening, arms crossed and nodding his head like some sage. I remember these moments because it's when I was talking about Temi that I was realising more and more just how much I was feeling her. Like, for example, I hate ultra-processed food, I think I said that, but my weakness is that Butterkist toffee popcorn. And you know sometimes you're eating something and the dopamine is hitting? So the more you eat it, the more you're like, fuck, man, I proper love these. Yeah, true, after a while you'll feel sick, but as I said – well, actually, as King Jaffe Joffer said – *there's a fine line*, get me.

Chapter 8

After my shift I linked up with Ross for a back and biceps session. This was the first one I'd be doing which included some of my new period of training – basically a lot more reps and high-intensity cardio to burn off the fat. The receptionist that day was one girl called Carli I moved to once, and after we beat and I locked it off. She'd been cold with man ever since but today she seemed calm. She looked good too, lip gloss on and her gym shirt tied up at the bottom so it was tighter on her chest. I looked at her breasts when I walked in and was instantly thinking about Temi. She had me, boy, couldn't check for no other gyal. I looked up into Carli's eyes and she had on one of those smiles. One of them where I knew she thought I was missing her and was regretting what I'd lost. Was happy to let her think what she wanted, to be honest. If you're happy then I'm happy, get me, let everyone do their own ting.

Anyway, the gym was busy. All the treadmills

were taken by those corporate types and there were teenagers from the college close to the gym cheering on their boy tryna shoulder press 18kg. I'm on the gym floor now and I'm telling Ross about the party and how fucked I felt in the morning, how I nearly messed up my diet. Basically, I was thinking my stomach was chatting shit because really it wanted to eat all that junk food in the kitchen. I think I've already said that I don't really drink like that, and even Ross was surprised. Nah, actually, he wasn't surprised about the drinking, he was surprised I was saying I was in love. It even sounded weird to me coming out my mouth.

'You say this now,' Ross said, 'but give it a few weeks and she'll be looking at you the same way as Carli, poor thing.'

'Why you acting like you care?' I said.

'I care, mate, I just don't tell you about it. Carli was a good girl.'

'Was?'

'Well she told me she's never dating again.'

'Everyone says that. I only beat once, man, stop trying to stir shit.'

'I'm just saying, mate.'

'Ross, man, you're helping me too much.'

I was doing pull-ups while we were chatting. He was only supposed to be there with his hands under my lats just in case I needed a bit of help. But I could feel his hands during every rep. This is what I'm saying. It's not a big deal with high reps, but still, it's annoying. I told him to move away from me and managed to do ten more. When I dropped and turned around to him, he looked a bit upset that I told him to move from me. I won't lie, I felt bad. I'm swayed way too easily, man. Ross was cool peoples as well, and we'd been training together since the squash court got refurbished into a swimming pool. He was similar to me in that he wasn't trying to settle down with anyone. Well, like how I used to be. And at one point, I can't remember when, we had a competition to see who could beat the most girls in the gym. I know this sounds mad but it wasn't even like that. We're all adults, innit, and if we want to have sex, we will. Nothing wrong with that. So if I move to you and tell you what I'm on and you're on it too, then there's no wrongdoing, alie? That's how I moved. Ross was different. He had all these tactics he'd practise to try and get girls, like that Neuro-Linguistic Programming shit he used to try and tell me about, and I know he probably tried to use it on me as well. I don't even know why he needed all that shit because he wasn't ugly, like, he was genuinely handsome and probably had the biggest chest and arms in the gym. If anything, I reckon his goatee put people off. You know them ones where it's like a kid tried to draw a border round your mouth? I swear he looked like a bald version of that wrestler Buff Bagwell. Mad. Anyway, Ross was still training for hypertrophy, muscle growth, so after my set, he wrapped his weight belt around him with a 25kg plate and went for twelve. Do you think I even touched him? I encouraged him but didn't touch nothing, and he got out that last rep with so much satisfaction that he threw off the belt afterward and stepped to me like he wanted to throw hands.

'Bruv, move, man,' I said.

'Do your set then.'

'I'm resting.'

'You started that book yet?'

'You gonna be asking me this every other day?'

'Just answer the question you bellend.'

'Nah, I haven't.'

'What's stopping you?'

'I don't need to learn how to get women.'

'You ain't settling down, Ray, remember I said it.'

'Alright, last set.'

I went up and managed to get twenty-seven reps, and for once my arms looked bigger than

43

Ross's. I flexed my forearms and he pushed out his bottom lip and started nodding. He approved.

'You're going to miss this type of training,' he said.

'I'll still get pumped,' I said.

'Not like this you won't.'

'Patience. Eventually it'll all come back.'

'I still think it's fucking stupid.'

'Look, if it doesn't work, then it doesn't work. But I don't see why it wouldn't.'

'Because you're not gonna have any strength, you fucking bellend.'

'I *will* have strength.'

'You're gonna look like you've just run a marathon. I'll fucking say it again, you need body fat. You're gonna make yourself ill, Ray.'

'The body doesn't need fat. Who said that?'

'Any doctor you speak to, mate.'

'I'll be fine.'

Ross was finishing his last exercise when I saw Temi at the other end of the gym. She looked like she was walking out of a bright light, and I swear when she appeared the music in the gym stopped. I heard a weight drop like someone just abandoned their set to watch her passing through. Ross didn't even notice, and after his final rep said he'd see me tomorrow for shoulders and triceps. Honestly, I was glad, because I knew he'd start chatting shit if he saw her. He might even feel a bit jealous. Some man do, it's normal. But I didn't want him talking about Temi like she was just some any girl to 'programme' or dash away after having sex. I'd told her to meet me at the gym because that's where I spent most my time. Gym and the hotel. Honestly, when you're linking someone, I think it's better to just bring them into your world. Acting like you wanna go cinema and restaurant and all that is just long if you don't normally do it. Fake environment ain't gonna help you get to know someone, get me? So yeah, we were gonna do full-body even though I'd just done back. But I knew how to style it in a way where I wasn't hitting the same muscles in the muscle group I'd just worked, if that makes sense.

Chapter 9

I remember all this not just because it was the day after I'd met Temi and it was basically our first date. But because I think love needs confirmation in real life. Like, you can feel it on the inside but there needs to be some external validation, get me. And for me, one thing came straight after the other. So on the treadmill we warmed up for ten minutes, light jogging speed next to each other, and we could even talk, that's how slow we were going. I jumped off first and she followed me, so it felt like I was leading. Leading the session, I mean. But like I said, Temi weren't no beginner, but I think because this was my home gym she didn't wanna move like she knew more than I did. To be honest, though, at this point, she could have. We squatted, four sets of twenty-five reps, shoulder press the same, chest press machine and then wide-grip lat pulldown. This is where I needed to be careful and adjust my form so I wasn't doubling up on hitting specific muscles. When she sat down to do her set, I watched her back. I didn't feel nothing sexual or anything, but more like this aesthetic pleasure. See, women who go gym, their backs usually look better to me than men's. Obviously men's backs can hold more muscles, but at a certain point it just looks too much, like just bare meat packed into one space. But with women, you can see the muscle, and it looks like there could be more but it's not necessary. Holding back. This is what I'm saying – restraint looks and feels good. Anyway, after her last on the pulldown, I said we should try some deadlifts but she wasn't on it. I was surprised.

'We should have done that first if we were gonna do it,' she said.

'Yeah, true, but it doesn't really matter if we're not gonna be lifting heavy.'

'It does for me.'

'Aight, let's do something else then.'

'Can we? Sorry, it's just my lower back.'

'Nah, it's calm. I'm just tryna think of another compound exercise.'

'Actually, fuck it, let's do it.'

'Fuck it, yeah?

'Shut up.'

'You sure?'

'Yeah, let's just do it. I said I'll follow your plan so . . .'

'Aight, cool.'

I made sure we didn't stack the weight so even when we got to twenty-five reps we'd still feel like we could do at least ten more. Couldn't be mashing up gyal on the first date, them waking up aching in the morning and associating that feeling with me. Our rest periods were longer too, to the point where the session started to feel like a write-off. Which was calm. We could talk. And I liked talking to her.

'So what's your training like?' I said.

'I usually just do whatever I feel like doing that day,' she said.

'And you still look like this?'

'I'm not lazy, Ray. I just don't have a plan.'

'Okay, fair, fair. And what's your diet like?'

'I eat whatever I want.'

'I knew you were going to say that.'

'Well it's true. But I don't really like processed food that much so maybe that helps.'

'Helps a lot. I saw you eating bare protein at Jeremy's house.'

'Why were you guys just sitting and watching what people were eating?'

'We were just chatting in that corner and could see people. We weren't tryna watch people like that.'

'Except you did . . .'

'Yeah . . .'

'Is it my set?'

'Nah, it's mine.' I stepped forward and started my reps, but all I could think about was finishing this conversation. So I was moving a bit faster than I normally would. I didn't care for my technique either. I just needed to get it done and then let her do hers.

'Can I ask you something?' I said, once she'd done her last rep. I probably should have waited for her to at least chill for a few seconds. But it felt like the longer things were left as they were, the worse it might be later to bring it up again.

'Yeah,' she said.

'Are you one of those people who don't like it when people watch you eat?'

'What do you mean?'

'You know like how some people don't like eating in front of people. I'm not sure why. Maybe they're embarrassed to be chewing or something.'

'Right.'

'So?'

'No, I don't mind people seeing me eat. But watching me eat is something different. If I'm eating and you're not and you're just there watching the food going into my mouth, then why would I like that?'

'Okay, fair. I see what you're saying.'

'Yeah.'

'That's not what I was doing, though.'

'Do you remember what I had on my plate?'

'No.'

'Don't lie.'

'Okay, yeah, but only because I wanted to see if we liked the same food.'

'How old are you, Ray?'

'You're asking me now?'

'Yeah, because I thought we were the same age but I'm not so sure.'

'I'm twenty-four.'

'Right. Okay.'

'How old are you?'

'Older.'

'Is that an issue?'

'Probably not. Do you train like this every day?'

'Most days, yeah. I used to be more into hypertrophy, putting on muscle, I mean.'

'I know what hypertrophy means.'

'Okay?'

'I'm just saying.'

'Anyway, now I'm trying to lose as much fat as possible. I'll lose muscle too, but once I'm down to about one per cent body fat, I'm going to build pure muscle and maintain that body fat percentage as I get bigger.'

'How big do you want to get?'

'Have you seen *Fight Club*?' After I said this, she let out some big sigh before she answered me and said 'yes'. I'm not gonna lie, I was starting to think she was sly mocking man by the way she was chatting to me. But then, why come all this way to check me and train with me if you're just gonna take the piss?

'I'm not saying I love the film,' I said.

'But you want to look like Brad Pitt.'

'Why you saying it like that?'

'Like what?'

'Like this is some shit you've heard before.'

'Are you for real?

'Yes.'

'Okay, sorry. Go on.'

'I don't want to look like him. I want that same body aesthetic but more muscle.'

'Okay.'

'Yeah, I think I can do it in about two years.'

'A two-year plan. So you know exactly what you're going to do?'

'Yup. Know the food I'm gonna eat and the training I'm going to do. Honestly, though, if you don't keep switching up your training, you're just gonna end up bored.'

'I agree with that, actually.'

'So yeah, getting rid of all body fat then building up from there.'

'Descartes of gym.'

'I like that, actually. I know you're trying to take the piss but whatever.'

'I'm not even. You know who Descartes is?'

'Yes.'

'Who is he?'

'Rah, you really think I'm stupid, innit?'

'I don't. I'm just asking a question and you're getting defensive, Ray.'

'Why does it even matter?'

'Honestly, it doesn't.'

'Aight, if I know who he is, you choose the next date.'

'The next date?'

'Yeah. Obviously I'd like to see you again. You surprised?'

'A little. Okay, next date is on me.'

'Okay, cool.'

'Well?' she asked.

'He's a French philosopher. *Cogito, ergo sum.*'

'Meaning?'

'"I think, therefore I am."'

'Where did you learn that?'

'One book about unleashing your potential, I think. Or something about philosophers. Why?'

'So you know who Descartes is but you don't know what a novel is?'
'What you chatting about?'
'Nothing. Okay, when am I seeing you?'
'Tomorrow. I'll meet you at my hotel.'

Chapter 10

Temi called my hotel a 'dive'. But it was okay, she said, 'I love a dive.' The next day when she came to check me at work, I was upstairs and I said we should stay in one of the rooms. She didn't even answer me, just walked back to the lift and pressed the button to go down.

'You think I'm just trying to beat, innit?' I said.

'I don't know what to think yet,' she said.

We walked up and down the high road just talking and walking into a shop every now and then to see what it was saying. Not really trying to buy anything. It was around those times when it takes long to get dark but the atmosphere still feels like it should be. Weren't really a lot of people about but I was a bit shook we'd bump into someone from work. I made sure I didn't show no one who Temi was, and I'm sure Omar, who was on shift with me, just thought she was a customer. Even when we'd walked out of the hotel together and I looked back, he didn't seem to notice. Or maybe he just didn't care, Omar was never really up in people's business like that. Anyway, as we were walking, Temi told me about the novel she was writing, about how one day she wanted to be able to make enough Ps from it that she didn't have to write the obituaries anymore. She loved doing it, she said, 'I think I told you that. But it's exhausting writing about people who are no longer here, and sometimes I get carried away.' She wouldn't give me the details of what she was writing about in her novel but she said she was interested in the lives of Black men. I was just like yeah, I hear you. I didn't really get it to be honest, because if she was interested in Black men, just chill with them. Why did she need to write about them? I didn't say this, though. Instead, I said something like:

'I never really understood storybooks,' I confessed. 'Like, what's the point of them?'

'There are quite a few answers to that question, but I think these days it's to be entertained. The same way people go to the cinema.'

'But everything's just in your head, though.'

'Yeah?'

'I dunno. Just sounds stressful having to do all that work when you can go cinema or listen to music. How much could you make from one book?'

'Again, there's many answers. But usually not a lot. How much money is there in hotels?'

'You think this is a job I wanna do for the rest of my life?'

'No? So what do you want to do then?'

'Nutritionist.'

The funny thing about love is that it comes and goes but people chat about it like it's forever. I didn't really notice this until I started fucking with Temi. Yeah, you don't always feel it, but inside of it, and what it's left inside of you, there are other things like hope and fascination. Things like respect that keep it alive, if you get me. So for example, sometimes I'd wake up and not feel like I loved Temi. I'd feel like I liked her or respected her, wanted to be around her. But not that intense love feeling. But there was always still this feeling that I knew it would come back. And it always did. Sometimes at random times, like watching her walk or hearing her tell me about one book or something she was writing. Or even just watching her writing, looking up at me in my face like say I was her inspiration. Or other times I could just sit down for a while thinking about her and then it'd be there, that feeling of love.

Chapter 11

Listen, Temi wasn't joking when she said she loved 'dive' hotels. Reminded her of life having been lived, she said. Probably something to do with her job, I dunno, but I kinda sensed that she didn't want to bring me to her house yet. We'd be going for a walk somewhere so I could get my steps in, and whenever we passed some bruk-down hotel, sometimes just looking like a house someone had tried switch up, she'd be like 'let's stay there'. She'd walk around each place looking for 'quirks', that's what she called them, but I saw them as whatever was mash up about the place. One room we stayed in basically had camping beds for us to sleep on. We pushed them together but the bars the coils were attached to kept bruising me in my sleep, so I just slept on the floor. When I woke up, Temi was lying next to me and the two camping beds were pushed into one corner.

A next place was basically a school. We had to walk for about four minutes before we got to our room. And it was in some massive inside 'courtyard', which I know used to be a basketball court. Opposite our room, like way opposite, were other rooms, and if you looked around it properly, there was a climbing frame thing in the corner. Temi said we should try and get up it but I weren't on it so I just watched her try and climb it in her silk pyjamas at 2 a.m. I was supposed to keep watch in case someone came through, but I was just watching her backoff. When she got down, I remember kissing her hard. So hard, to the point when she opened her mouth to put her tongue in mine, our teeth clashed and she gently pushed me back a bit. I was too eager. She didn't mind, though, I noticed, she'd just correct me and then we'd carry on. We ended up having sex out there, outside our room in that basketball court hotel. After that was the first time she told me she loved me.

In the morning, while we were trekking back to the reception area, I clocked how the carpets looked like those ones Irishmen used to sell door-to-door back in ends. Temi took a picture of it but I was just eager to leave. Bare artefacts from my childhood in one place was just too much. But there was one hotel I genuinely liked even though it was dirty. Dirty to the point when you tried to rub a finger over the skirting board it moved bare slow because everything had become sticky. Dirty to the point even the cobwebs were dusty and looked so old you know the spiders died out time ago. But there was a kitchen in the room and it was only like thirty-five pounds a night. And there was a proper oven, stovetop, grill, decent countertop and all that. The oven was even better than the one at Temi's yard. Only mad thing about it was that it was gas. And after what I told Temi about people coming through to hang themselves, it was obvious what I was gonna say about this as well.

'You're really morbid sometimes,' she said.

'Am I?' I said.

'Yeah. Stop it. It's not sexy.'

'You don't think writing about people dying is morbid?'

'That's not what I do and you know that, so I don't know why you're framing it like that.'

'I'm joking, man, chill.'

'Yeah, you're so funny. Should we try and cook something?'

'I'm down.'

'Your packed lunch, though?'

'I'll eat it for breakfast. There's a Tesco down the road. Their rump steak is decent.'

We had steak and sweet potatoes, spinach, watercress and rocket, rice cakes and strawberry jam for dessert.

When we checked out in the morning, there was a guy sitting outside the hotel asking for change. I gave him my prepped meal. He said it'd be cold. *Yeah, I hear it*, I thought. So I went back inside the hotel and told them the oven in the room wasn't working this morning so could they just warm my food for me. *I know the rules but please, I'm hungry and it's the faulty room's fault.* The guy at reception was vex, I could tell, but did it anyway. *I ain't gonna sue you if it burns my tongue, don't worry*, I said, or thought, and thanked him and walked back out to the guy sitting out in front. I gave him the food and a piece of cutlery I always keep with me too.

'What is it?' he asked.

'Rump steak and sweet potatoes,' I said, then took Temi's hand and walked off before he could thank me. If he was going to, I mean. I don't like being thanked for stuff like that. Makes me uncomfortable. Anyway, when we got to the bus stop Temi squeezed my hand and pulled me into her face, kissed my lips softly and then wiped the gloss off my lips.

'You're a good egg,' she said. I hadn't had eggs in time, I thought, and tried to calculate the amount of calories in five if I decided to have them for breakfast instead.

We did eventually stay for a night in my hotel, though. On the day I booked it, I was trying hard to remember which rooms I had stayed in before with different girls. I didn't wanna disrespect the ting by taking Temi to one of the same rooms. This wasn't normal procedure, though, staying in the hotel you worked in. If you had to do a night shift and then a morning shift because there wasn't enough staff or someone was sick or something, then you could. But on a normal one, it wasn't allowed. But Ruby was cool like that. She'd see you emailing head office about booking a room at discount and she'd just drop one 'humph' and turn away. You'd have to make up for it, though, like later on she'd ask you to do something that she knew you didn't wanna do. But she allowed you, so now you gotta pay up somehow.

But yeah, I was stressing over finding a room, but luckily, or maybe not, because it was a bit weird, but Omar told me I'd never stayed in room 817.

'How do you know that?' I said.
'Because I notice,' he said.
'Yeah, obviously, but why?'

'You think I wanna sleep in a bed where I know you been with a woman?'

Me and Temi didn't have sex the first time we stayed there. We just sat on the bed eating junk food and watching movies. Well, she was eating the junk food, I was picking up packs of random shit and reading the ingredients. It's mad what's allowed to be put in food. I had some raspberries and blueberries, a little pot of organic Greek yoghurt as well. Temi's stomach was proper flat when she was laying down, and she was picking at some of the tiny hairs just below her belly button. I felt like this was a test. To see if I could control myself. But we know the deal. Discipline ain't nothing to me. Anyway, we were watching the *Bourne* trilogy. It was her idea, actually, and I thought she was just trying to pick something she thought I'd like. But it got to the point where I'd say a line that was coming up, and then she would say a another one. And then we'd both look at each other and say in unison, 'Jesus Christ, that's Jason Bourne!'

'I used to love watching films like this with my dad, man,' I said, after we'd stopped giggling over our nonsense.

'That's cute,' she said.

'How come you're into this stuff?'

'Pause it. How come I'm into this stuff? Why not?'

'I'm not saying you can't be or anything. But I dunno, it's just not something I expected, get me?'

'I love anything that's good, that's it really.'

'Yeah, me too. What's a film you could watch over and over and not get bored?'

'Probably this. And *Casino Royale*. I love *Leaving Las Vegas* as well.'

'I've never heard of that one.'

'I don't think you'd like it,' she said.

'Anything else? I'm gonna watch everything you mention.'

'I think that's it, really. Maybe *Eternal Sunshine* as well.'

'Okay, cool. I'll watch them all. I'll tell you what I think.'

'You don't have to.'

'I know I don't.'

'What films did you watch with your dad?'

'Mostly action movies, to be honest. We couldn't go cinema so we'd have like these movie nights. Bare popcorn and sweets. We used to watch *Commando* a lot. *Matilda*. *Demolition Man*. *Coming to America*. *Boomerang*. *Last Action Hero*. We watched *Fight Club* together, too.'

'Did your dad like it?'

'I don't even know if he liked any of them. He only watched them because of me. I know he loved *Tom and Jerry*, though.'

'That's actually so random.'

'Innit? I'd catch him watching it by himself and bussing up.'

'Cute. So when did you decide to be like Brad Pitt.'

'Stop saying that, man. I don't want to be like him.'

'Sorry. Yeah, the shape of his body.'

'Yeah. You make it sound so weird.'

'I don't think it's weird at all. If I'm honest, it was a little off-putting when you first said it, though.'

'Why?'

'Just is.'

'Alright.'

'So?'

'What?'

'When did you know you wanted to?'

'I've always liked that body type, like the lean look. My genetics are weird, though. I don't do much and suddenly I'm hench. But it ain't all muscle. So I've just got to strip all the fat off my body and then slowly build back up with just muscle. My dad used to say I was a bit too fat as well. Not *fat* fat, but like I had bits of fat.

He wasn't being mean or anything, my dad was calm, but he'd catch me opening a second bag of popcorn like forty minutes into a film and tell me to tek time. See this bit of fat here on my waist?' I pinched it with four fingers on the bottom and my thumb on top. 'You see all this, I didn't even clock it was there when I was young. My dad grabbed it and showed me one time. He grabbed his own bit of wrinkly flab too, so I didn't feel bad about it. I'll never forget that. It looked like the fat on his body was being held like water in some crumpled black plastic bag or something. But yeah, he said I'm too young for it. For that kinda fat, I mean. I'm glad he showed me, though, because that's the hardest part of body fat to lose. It's better you're aware because you gotta put in bare work.'

Temi was listening and didn't say anything until she stretched past me, reached her hand over my stomach to grab some sweets and I flinched just a small piece. She noticed. She gave me this look as if I misunderstood something.

'I wasn't going to touch you,' she said.

'I know,' I said.

'Hmmm. Okay.'

'Nah, seriously.'

'Alright. Well, I do think that's a lot for a dad to do. But I guess only you know him and his intentions. But isn't that dangerous? Having no fat?'

'Everyone keeps saying this but I don't think it is. I'll be doing it slowly, like maybe losing 15lbs a month. I'll still have some muscle on my body, just not loads.'

'15lbs is a lot, Ray.'

'It is, but trust me, I'll be getting all the nutrients, all the fibre. I have it planned out.'

'Alright. It's your body but be careful.'

'I will.'

'Will be interesting to see.'

'Trust me. Just watch.'

Part 2

Chapter 1

140lbs

One of the hardest things about trying to drop weight is how much meal prep you gotta do and how expensive it can be. True, when I was doing a normal cut or bulking, I still had to meal-prep. But during those times I could slip up or miss couple days and it would be a minor. But I couldn't do that with the new programme I was running. It had been six months since I started and I was finally down to around 10 stone. I'd put in work. And my body fat was about 9 per cent as well. There was one morning when I was food-prepping and it was taking me bare long to do everything. I'd prep for Temi sometimes too, link her on the way to work. She loved my cooking and I know she loved seeing me grinning bare teet in the morning as well. But that morning it was just me, and I remember being so tired.

That's another thing that's hard about dropping

weight. You're always tired, fam. Like, not even in a yawning lemme-go-find-my-bed kinda way. In a I-feel-like-I'm-gonna-drop-dead-any-minute kind of way. I felt like a zombie, fam, it was nuts. Then I'd eat and feel lively for about two hours until I felt hungry again. I say hungry, but the feeling wasn't really like feeling hunger anymore. It was more like my body was switching on me or something. Fiending for food it didn't even need.

But yeah, one morning I'm prepping my food, got the grill heating and I'm cutting up steak pieces of venison. Listen, venison was a cheat code for dieting – 200 grams of it was like 200 calories, no fat on it at all. So sometimes I'd have that three times a day with raspberries and that would only be about 1,000 calories with bare protein and enough fibre. At first I was worried about how my stomach was gonna start moving but it was fine, really. Sometimes I would switch up the berries for some cannellini beans. Only 240 calories in a can. Kept in water, obviously. But I could only have that maybe once a day with the venison or lean-cut rump steak. Bare red meat, I know. But because I was having nuff fruit and blending my watercress, spinach and rocket, I was basically cancelling out the bowel issues, get me. Or I'd just back some chia seeds throughout the day. So yeah, cutting up the venison was taking bare long. My arms felt bare heavy and I just wanted to get back into bed. I could have called in sick and I know Ruby wouldn't mind but the hotel was busy. I felt bad leaving them man like that when I was just tired. Everybody gets tired, man, so I needed to fix up. I packed up my food, blended my veg and fruit, poured that in a flask, and was out the door. I'd already weighed myself that morning. I would always do it first thing. Better if I could go toilet before but I couldn't always make that happen when I needed it.

So yeah, the next thing I remember I'm walking up the high road now and feeling like I was on something. By these times I was semi-used to the tiredness so I couldn't figure out why I was feeling so mashed. I couldn't even see lights properly; cars were coming like they were just a blur on some painted canvas. That's how the world was looking to me: like something created and not real, like someone tried to recreate what I was seeing but couldn't get the realism right. My belly started rumbling, chatting shit to me, and that's when I finally realised: I forgot to have breakfast. I swear down, once I realised that, things started to feel and look normal again. It was like the world decided to move mad just to get me to remember I hadn't eaten. I stopped in the middle of the street, opened my bag and took out one container of my food and a fork. I didn't care, I was gonna walk and eat that shit on the street. People walk on road eating chicken with their hands, so why would they care if I was using a fork. But I didn't, I didn't start eating, because then my meals for the day would be fucked and no way I'm eating any ultra-processed food. Even in an emergency. The thing about those UPFs is that even if the calories are low, they still fuck with your hormones and can make your body store food as fat instead of using it as energy. Trust me, it'll even store it in the most annoying places. Even at 10 stone, I still had one chunk of fat on my lower stomach that I could grab, that wouldn't fucking go. Used to proper piss man off, but I knew it was because I had been eating crap food for how many years. Anyway, so yeah, I thought *nah, I can't even eat this now*. I put it back in my bag and decided to firm it until it was time for lunch. Let my stomach chat shit. It'll thank me later when it's free from all that fat. Anyway, I'm saying all this just to show you wagwan, show you how hard it was. I put in mad work.

When I stepped out the lift now, I saw the back of this guy's head looking like it was balancing on his trap muscles. I knew straight away who it was. But why was Ross there? I walked slowly past him, watching him all the way like I was circling him, and when he saw me he started grinning teet. What did this guy want?

'There he is,' he said.

'Yeah, wagwan?' I said.

'You satisfied now?' Ross said to Omar behind the reception. He was standing there with his arms folded and legs apart.

'What's going on?' I said to them both.

'Nothing. Your boy was waiting for you,' said Omar, and walked around the corner to the bar, obviously just to get away from whatever was happening because he didn't serve drinks.

'Ross, wagwan, man?' I said. He stepped closer to me as I was putting in the code to the reception door, so I stopped and waited for him to say something.

'You couldn't sort me out a room, could you?'

'Is that why you're here?'

'Yeah, that and to see where the fuck you been.' Man was feeling confident now because he knew I could get him the room.

'I've just been here, man.'

'You look like you've just run a marathon.'

'Shut up, man. Let me put my shit down. I'll book your room for you, wait there.'

'Legend.'

Ruby was sitting in front of her computer

checking customer reviews. I was just about to ask if I could use her computer to book my boy Ross, but she said she heard it all and had sent the email to central room booking already.

'You going to clean out the fridge today,' she said.

'Ah, Ruby, please, allow it,' I said.

'There's no "*Ruby please*" today. Clean it before your next room check.'

I was pissed. That fridge hadn't been cleaned out for time and smelled like sour milk. I'd have to hold my breath and take breaks every thirty seconds. Fucking Ross, you know. I went out and told him the room was booked.

'I haven't even told you when I want it for yet,' he said.

'My manager heard you. She booked it.'

'Lovely. So where you been then?'

'I've just been running mostly.'

'You're gonna lose everything, mate.'

'Nah, I do pull-ups and press-ups. It doesn't even matter because I'm gonna get it all back.'

'Like fuck you are. Come to the gym tomorrow.'

'Can't tomorrow. But I will soon. Maybe couple weeks or something. Work's mad busy. I'll bell you, though.'

'Yeah, alright. What time?'

Chapter 2

135lbs

Without even asking if I was cool with it, Ross brought through one of his friends to train with us. His name was Kofi. Ghanaian, obviously, though man had long braids, and was leaner than me but with more muscle. All that is probably why Ross asked him to roll with us, as if he would give me inspiration or something. Listen, Ross was always talking about inspiration, he was one of those talkers where as soon as he sees someone walking past or getting close, he turns his voice up. He thinks everyone is looking to hear whatever shit he's chatting. I think everyone cares about his little community views. True, I won't lie, though, sometimes when we were lifting together, he managed to talk me into lifting heavier than I thought I could. And I did learn some discipline from him. But more time what he'd be talking about was gyal and how to draw them, how to manipulate them and all that. How the world's becoming more 'gyno centric', whatever that even means. He don't rate them except for their bodies. And he told me once that even with rating their bodies, there is no such thing as a 10. I remember thinking, *if this Kofi brudda is on this stuff, then I'm just gonna be there paying for two man's headache.* Two grown man chatting shit about if I wanna achieve my goals, I need to let go of my girl. Long.

Anyway, we decided on a chest session but it became long very quickly. Kofi and I could only lift a certain amount and Ross was getting vex because his energy was being taken up having to take plates on and off the bar.

'Well this was a bad fucking idea,' he said.

'See why I weren't coming gym?' I said.

'Yeah, I see. Bloody liar,' he said.

'How am I lying,' I said.

'How's Termi?' he said.

'Temi. She's fine. Why?' I'm not gonna lie, even him saying her name made me get a little heated. I knew where he was gonna try to go with this and I wasn't having it. I was too tired to care about getting into beef. One thing I'll say about this mad fatigue is that things don't seem to matter anymore. That feeling of being in a dream can affect your decisions. So at times like this, I liked it.

'Just asking,' he said.

'Speak with your chest, bro,' I said.

'You guys chill,' said Kofi. He'd just been there watching us and checking his phone for his next set. Probably realised we'd end up talking through our rest period so needed to break it up.

'Fuck this,' Ross said, 'I'll meet you boys in the steam room. I'm not gonna get much done helping you two with your baby weights.' He walked off and I honestly felt my body find itself back on the ground. It was like the more vex I became, the more I slightly lifted myself off the floor without even realising it. I must have been on tiptoes at some point.

'I think he's pissed you dropped him out for your girlfriend,' Kofi said.

'What are you even chatting about? I didn't drop anyone out for anyone,' I said. Who the fuck was this guy talking like he knew what was going on?

'Well, he told me that's why he's pissed off. He thinks your girlfriend told you to switch up your plan and stop going to the gym with him earlier because of some book?'

Yeah, I'd forgotten all about that. But Temi didn't say I should stop rolling with him, she just said she didn't like him. Basically what happened was she came to the hotel to link me one day. It was supposed to be a surprise because she'd noticed I was looking low. Those were her words, not mine. So she came through when she knew it would be quiet and leaned over the reception desk and called me. I was happy to see her but she caught me reading. She asked me what it was and I said just some book Ross gave me and she was like 'lemme see'. So I showed it to her and her face changed, boy. Personally, I don't really like showing people what I'm reading or talking about it. It's something I like keeping to myself, get me. Like, I don't judge people who like discussing their books and all that, like book clubs and shit like that. That's just not for me. I'm spending proper intimate time with the book and I ain't trying to share that with just anybody. More time nobody.

'Why are you reading this?' she said.

'Ross gave it to me,' I said.

'It's bullshit.'

'Why?'

'Because it is.'

'Have you read it?'

'I've read about it . . . and since when do *you* read, anyway?'

'I always read.'

'When?'

'When I'm on my ones. Sometimes before I go bed. Here at work. I don't like reading in public. It's like eating in public, makes me uncomfortable.'

'Makes you uncomfortable, why? Reading in secret.'

'It's not a secret. I just don't like chatting about it. There's bare stuff I don't know about you but you ain't keeping it secret, it just ain't come up or you don't like talking about it, alie?'

'But this has come up. Loads of times.'

'How?"

'Ray, I talk about what I'm reading and writing all the time and you don't say anything.'

'Yeah, because that's you, innit. Is this serious? It feels dumb.'

'I wanted to get some food with you.'

'Sorry. I can't leave yet.'

'Can I have something to eat here then?'

'You sure?'

'I'm not like you, Ray, I don't care.'

I asked chef to make her whatever she wanted and I'd cover him for an extra thirty minutes while on his break. He made her scrambled eggs with pieces of ham in it. When I saw Temi eating it, I couldn't even fix my face. Those eggs came out of cartons and the ham is so processed you might as well be eating soft plastic. Even thinking about it was making my stomach hurt. Temi was beautiful. Her lips were full and brown, with a little bit of red spilling over from the inside of her mouth onto her bottom lip. Her eyes so small so it looked like she was always focused on you. Body was banging, as I showed you before, and her skin was dark with a few scars here and there from chickenpox that made her unique. I loved her a lot and I know she knew that. So I don't know why she got so pissed off when, after she'd finished munching that nasty food, I turned my head away from kissing her goodbye.

Anyway, after that she wasn't feeling Ross, and any time I said I was going gym with him she'd kiss her teeth. Like an idiot I told Ross she didn't rate him, and at the time he just kinda brushed it off, but obviously it must have made it look like I was avoiding him.

I said to Kofi, nah, that's not it at all, and then explained to him my fitness journey and what I was trying to achieve, but how I was just more tired than I expected. He rated it, still, and said too many of us are only focused on looking hench for gyal or next man. That they don't care about how they look to themselves. The world is too focused on trying to please women, he said. Listen, the way I was nodding my head when he said that, because what's the point in showing off abs to your boys? Kofi was on some sage antics, though, like, when he spoke, it always sounded like he was dropping some wisdom without forcing it. Like, if you asked him certain kinds of questions, he'd be silent for a while before answering. Man measured his words like food and decided what was worth opening his mouth for. We had a couple things in common, nothing deep, though, like both Ghanaian, dark-skinned, short, those surface-level kinda things. He was from Accra, but my fam was from Kumasi, even though we both understood Twi. But also, we both had older parents. Like, my dad was about sixty when I was born and my mum forty-something. My mum don't leave her room, though. Just ordering shit and hoarding. Britain really is the land of gold to that generation. Anything has value, apparently. Anyway, it's nice to meet people with things in common. Even if the familiarity only lasts for a sentence. He wasn't dieting like me or trying to strip all fat off his body, but he liked the lean look and loved cardio too, though hated the idea of having a belly like an uncle and so did I. So I took his number, and we started running together on days when we were both free and not too tired.

Chapter 3

130lbs

Around these times things started to get a bit hazier and I sometimes thought I'd dreamed stuff instead of experiencing it. The exhaustion was mad in itself. I wasn't sleeping well either and had to try taking bare different pills and herbal drinks (zero calories, obviously) to try get man to sleep. But one thing I do remember from those times is how my weight was moving and sometimes a few events or moments that were connected to that. Anyway, after I met Kofi for the first time, things just carried on like normal: work, see Temi, home workout, weigh myself and all that. I weighed myself every day. I think I already said that. But yeah, at the same time in one or two places. Either in Temi's bathroom or in my kitchen just in front of the fridge.

So one morning now, I was bent over, looking down at the scale in Temi's bathroom, and was finally at 130lbs. It had taken its time, I can't lie, and I was even a bit shook that my body had completely adjusted to my low-calorie diet and I'd have to go even lower. Which was light work, I didn't mind, but like I said, I was trying to do this slowly and safely, get me. Usually, the night before I would have dropped one, two laxatives. Not them hardcore ones, just those soft ones where they work overnight. But obviously I couldn't do that when I stayed over at Temi's. But even still, my stomach was moving a bit mad. I thought I must have trapped wind or something. I hadn't even eaten anything at that point, as well. Anyway, while I was stood on the scale, I heard Temi shout from the living room, what am I gonna wear this evening. This evening, I thought, what's happening this evening? I stepped off and walked into the living room and asked her wagwan.

She was cooking scrambled eggs on the stove.

'Don't worry,' she said, 'they're real eggs.' I think I rolled my eyes.

'What's happening tonight?' I said.

'The dinner party?' she replied.

'Ahhh, allow it, please. I'm tired.'

'Ray, you haven't met any of my friends.'

'Yeah, so? You haven't met any of my friends, either.'

'I've met Kofi.'

'You saw him once. It's not the same.'

'Are we really going to fight about this?'

'We're not fighting.'

'So we're going then, yeah?'

'Honestly, I'm tired.'

'So am I. We'll only stay for a bit then. I promise. Please, please, please.'

'Fucking hell, yeah, alright.' Temi stepped to my face and kissed me softly on the lips. Her mouth didn't smell like eggs but I still associated because they were there on the stove behind her. I didn't pull back, though.

'What time is it?' I said.

'We need to get there for seven,' she said.

'Cool.'

'Do you know what you're wearing?'

'No.'

'I'll find something for you, don't worry.'

'Yeah, thanks.'

Temi had me wearing some purple slim-fit silk shirt and these tight black Primark jeans. Luckily I had my own crep, some Clarks I'd been rocking for years but kept in good condition. I can't even remember what Temi was wearing but I know her perfume smelled like vanilla and roses, that one perfume she knew I loved. We had a small argument before we left because she saw me putting a container of food in my bag. What was weird about Temi sometimes was that she knew what I was on. She knew how serious I was about my ting, about my goals, but still it's like she tried to distract me. Or even sabotage? Nah, okay, I can't say sabotage. Anyway, she was in front of me chatting and waving my container around in her hand. *Watch when the food spills on your red dress*, I must have been thinking. Yes, that's it. She was wearing some red dress, body tight, bum looking mad and her arms on show. I feel like it could have been the same one I seen her rocking at Jeremy's house but I'm not really sure. Anyway, I let her talk and told her I hear her. I put the container back in the fridge and went toilet. I locked the bathroom door and just sat there on the toilet thinking. Obviously I couldn't get out of the dinner, but I knew I wouldn't want to eat their food. I dunno why it's normal to eat in a next person's house. My mum used to warn me against it, even, telling me you don't know where people's hands have been. It's true, man. Listen, I didn't even need to go toilet when I went in there. But see me needing it after thinking about all this stuff. I was feeling bare hot and could feel those little bits of sweat you know gonna be up under your armpit. When

I stepped out into the passage, Temi was now sitting, writing in her little book.

'Can I read that one day?' I said. Temi jumped. She closed the notebook so fast and put it at the bottom of her bag.

'You can read it. But not today. Can we go please?' she said.

'Yeah, come.'

We didn't speak much on the way there. I passed the time looking at people on the train and trying to guess their weight and body fat percentage. I tried to do it with myself sometimes just before letting Kofi get my proper percentage with callipers. Another trainer at the gym used to do this for me, one brudda called Marcus. But since I weren't there much, Kofi said he'd do it. Kofi weren't a personal trainer, though, but he'd done a degree in biomechanics. No idea what that was but it meant he knew how to use bare different fitness tools. And it was also why he was more into running than weights and getting bigger. I won't lie, sometimes I felt like a test subject when he was chatting to me about dieting and all that other stuff. I didn't mind, though. Man dropped bare knowledge.

Anyway, me and Temi got to the dinner party and it was actually calm. I knew how I'd get out of eating the food, even though it looked decent. In the middle there were short ribs (750 calories per rib), roast potatoes (300 calories per 100g), small lamb shanks (400 calories per 100g). You get what I'm saying, bare food and bare calories. At least it wasn't ultra-processed. But maybe the bread was. I couldn't tell if it was sourdough or not. There were names on chairs, which was annoying, because I wasn't sitting next to Temi. I know you could see from my face what I was thinking about all this. And I ended up sitting next to one brudda called Daniel Wolff. I dunno who Temi was sitting next to, but she was bussing bare convo and laughing. Good for her, innit, I thought, and tried to chat to Daniel. When I say chat to, I mean I tried to get some words in. Man was talking bare, even if I weren't looking at him, he'd carry on. When I did fully turn and make proper eye contact with him, what do you think happened? Yup, he just carried on, looking in man's eyes like he was onto me. And I'd just be like, *yeah, I hear you*. He was a writer as well. I think everyone at the table was a writer or something like that. They all had smug looks on their faces too. Daniel the most – looking at me over his glasses like he couldn't just lift his head up and see straight. Man looked sinister when he finally asked me something about myself.

'So what do you do?' Daniel said.

'Hospitality. A hotel,' I said.

'Oh nice. Which one?'

'Just some budget one.'

'You like it?'

'It's cool for now, yeah. The people are calm.'

'Are you here with Temi?' He nodded in her direction. Probably clocked because I kept looking over at her chatting to my man.

'Yeah. Her plus-one. So when is your book coming out?' I said, changing the subject because trying to talk about myself was making me feel off. And my stomach was feeling like long fingers were crushing it into a ball whenever there was an awkward silence.

'Next year, September. Not sure how to feel about it. Don't get me wrong, I'm proud of what I've written, just not sure how readers will respond to it.'

'What's it about?'

'It's autofiction.'

'What's that?'

'Basically turning my life into fiction.'

'Fair enough.'

'Temi writes autofiction, doesn't she?'

'Is it?'

'Ask her.'

'Yeah, I will.'

'So clearly not for you then?' Daniel said.

'Not really. I think, I think life means less if everyone knows about it, if you get what I mean?'

'I do.'

'Yeah. Like, special moments are special because they're personal.'

'Do you read much?'

'Yeah, sometimes.'

'What are you reading at the moment?

'Erm, *Meditations*. By Marcus Arelus.'

'I don't think I've read that. What's the story?'

'It's not a storybook. It's like philosophy. Life lessons and how to be stoic.'

'Oh right, yes, you mean Marcus *Aurelius*. I know who you mean now.'

'Yeah.' What a dickhead, I thought.

'So you're into philosophy and all that, are you? Who else have you read?'

'I'm into whatever, really. Just not stories. My friend recommended this. Before that I was reading *The Game* by Neil Strauss.'

'*The Game*?'

'Yeah, have you read it?'

'I haven't.'

'It's decent.'

'Have you read any of Temi's writing?'

'Nah, she won't let me. She talks about it, though, but I've not read it.'

'She sends me chapters of the book she's currently writing. Do you go to the gym much?'

'I used to. But not for a while. I mostly run and do stuff at home.'

'I see. Sorry, I just need to go find something.' He got up and walked over to Temi, interrupted her laugh and was saying something in her ear. By this time my stomach was actually hurting. I think I must have convinced my body to lie for me so I didn't need to eat. But it took man seriously. I felt like I'd suddenly become bare bloated, and my abs were cramping or something. I'd done mad crunches the day before, actually. You know when you're doing a set of something and you know you can do one more rep? But at the same time, you know that one more rep gonna mean pain the next day but you do it anyway? Yeah, so maybe man was suffering for the day before.

Temi sat down next to me and smiled.

'You okay?' she said.

'Yeah, I'm cool. What's wrong with my man?'

'Daniel? Nothing. He just asked me if I'd prefer to sit next to you. What was he saying to you?'

'Just chatting shit, really.'

'Ray, don't be rude please.'

'Aight, sorry.'

*

Everyone was reaching for the food and filling up their plates and I was just sitting there. The host, I forget her name, told me to help myself but I told her I ain't feeling too good, that my stomach was feeling tight and bloated. She offered me something but I said nah, I'm cool. And when I said this she recoiled, dropped into her chair like I told her to fuck off or something. I joined in the convos, though, like, I wasn't being antisocial. But Temi kept looking over at me from the corner of her eye but not saying anything. Bro, I was so tired I just wanted to go home. But I knew Temi wanted to be there so I was firming it. People were even getting tipsy and I hate talking to people who've been drinking when I haven't. Even Temi was starting to move annoying. Listen, there was some caviar left in the middle of the table and she put some on top of a piece of lamb and told me to try it. Nah, I'm good, I said. Trust me, try it. It's so nice, she said. She had it on a fork with her other hand underneath it, trying to move it toward my mouth like I was a baby.

'I'm good, Temi. Stop, man,' I said under my breath. People carried on their own convos but were looking over while talking.

'Ray, please just try it.'

'Temi, no!'

'You'll thank me, I promise.' The fork was nearly touching my lips and I could feel the room going quiet. So I held onto my stomach and bent forward, made some groaning sound and asked the host where the toilet was. I walked toward where she was pointing, looking back only once to see Temi. She was still sitting there with the fork in her hand. She looked like she was trying to feed a ghost.

We didn't talk on the way home. I was gonna say I'll go to my own yard and sleep but I remembered I was meeting Kofi in the area to jog in the morning. My stomach was still hurting, so when we got in, I just laid down on the sofa, my knees up to my chest. I didn't have any covers but I tried to sleep, anyway. I heard the kettle boiling. And after a few minutes, Temi was stood over me, watching. I looked up at her and said 'what?' She kneeled in front of me, stroked my forehead and then kissed me. I was thinking *wagwan for this girl, man?* Bare confusing. She stood up, taking my hand while she did, and pulled me up too, tell me to come to bed. I was still vex even if she wasn't. But I went with her, and she passed me a hot-water bottle as we walked toward her bedroom.

Chapter 4

125lbs

There were times when my weight would increase for no reason. I think it might have been because I wasn't sleeping well enough. So my body was holding onto too much water and sugar, Kofi said. My man knew his stuff. When my weight went up the first time, I tried fasting. I lasted a week. But lemme tell you, though, when I got to day five, I swear it felt like I could go on for another five. I dunno what it was but I felt so much peace, like, clarity and everything. That's when I knew I had to keep pushing forward. I knew I could do this, do like Descartes, as Temi said. We still weren't chatting properly but that was on her. I know she felt embarrassed because of what she did. Anyway, when I came off the fast, I'd dropped like 7lbs. I started drinking soup and blending my berries for fibre, slowly moving onto solid food. But my weight went up again. It was pissing me off, and this was when I started thinking maybe food trying to irritate me on purpose. I know it sounds mad. But say like when you knock your foot on something and you swear at the ting. And then it happens again and you're thinking this piece of whatever is trying to make me vex on purpose. It was something like that. So anyway, I thought the most important thing for man is the nutrients in food. So if I could get all the nutrients, but lower the calories, I'd be good. So I tried a ting. I started eating, waiting like an hour, then went into the toilet and got that shit out my belly. It made my stomach hurt even more, and I only did it a few times a week, but come see how my weight started dropping properly again.

Chapter 5

115lbs

I was jogging with Kofi and he was telling me about another philosopher called Schopenhauer. He never called them philosophers, though, he called them 'thinkers'. I never really got this, but I think it was because then he could be levels with them man. Anyway, I was telling him about my stomach. He'd seen it for himself because I kept having to stop and bend over. That was when I felt relief, like, that's when the bloating felt like it was going away. I knew it weren't my ab workouts at this point because I'd started allowing them a few weeks before. And the pain was still there. But Kofi was telling me how everyone suffers and how it's just part of being human. But how women suffer in different ways because they're built different. But even still, women can cause the suffering of man just because it's their nature.

Before this I'd never really listened to this kinda chat. Not about suffering, but about gyaldem hurting man and all that kinda stuff. But by this time, Temi hadn't spoken to me for around five weeks. Even though I'd be staying at her house sometimes, she'd just give me one-word answers like some child.

'Because they are basically children,' Kofi said.

'Yeah, I hear you,' I said.

'Don't get it twisted, I love women. I'm not gay or anything, but I know what they're like.'

'Yeah, I hear you.'

'Does Temi support you and your training?'

'Yeah, I can't lie, she does. To the point where sometimes if I've forgotten what I had to eat the day before, she'll remind me so I stay on track.'

'How does she know?'

'I dunno. I'm in her house so she probably just remembers.'

'Fair enough.'

'Yeah, when she's not being a bitch, she's actually calm.'

'Until being a bitch lasts longer and longer and then they can't pretend anymore. People's natures always show over time. Nothing we can do about it. Women can't help being who they are, get me?'

'Yeah, I hear you.' By this time I was thinking

about my own nature. I was wondering what I'm like to other people.

We carried on jogging with my stomach pain at intervals, and after a while, every time I stopped, Kofi would let out a breath louder than his heavy breathing.

Chapter 6

105lbs

I felt this sudden pain in my neck and lifted my head. I must have fallen asleep on Ruby's desk with my head flat sideways, nearly falling off the swivel chair. I heard Omar speaking in Arabic to one of the cleaners. And even though I couldn't see him, I could tell from the vim in his voice that his hands were moving about in the air. Man, I was so tired, but pushed myself out the chair and walked to reception to see wagwan. They were both quiet when they saw me like I was the one they were arguing about. Omar asked me if I was okay and Werda nodded. She couldn't speak English but I think she was agreeing with the question. I said I was fine, just tired. My body must have clocked the lie because my abs started hurting again. When I got to like 110lbs, the pain was basically permanent. But I was firming it, folding my body when I could. Because I knew if I went to see my GP or something they'd chat shit about what I was trying to achieve. Anyway, we were all standing there and they were both looking at me. I was closing my eyes hard to try and push back the pain. I must have bent over slightly because Werda came round to our side of reception and stood next to me. I felt like she was trying to make eye contact with me to communicate something. But I couldn't keep my eyes open long enough. Then I felt a hand on my shoulder and I was so shocked that my willpower overcame the pain for a few seconds. But when I looked up to confirm what I was thinking, Omar was closer to me as well.

Chapter 7

95lbs

There wasn't any massive argument or some big betrayal. One day when I was about 95lbs, Temi just told me she couldn't be with me anymore. I can't lie, I knew it was coming, so I could take it and act like it was nothing. She said some mad things about me too. Stuff I don't even like to think about because it wasn't true. But that's how women lie, I guess. Kofi tried to show man at the time but I wasn't listening. Minor. I was stoic about it and even that pissed her off.

'I want you to get better,' she said.

Better from what? Apparently, it wasn't fair what I was doing. Calm, whatever, just one more distraction gone. And I wouldn't have to eat at the same time as her anymore. All just controlling behaviour, anyway, and I didn't need that shit, get me.

Chapter 8

90lbs

It got to the point where I couldn't jog the way I used to. I was bare slow and even Kofi asked me wagwan. I used to have to slow down for man and now he was having to completely stop while I caught my breath or had to bend over and hold my stomach. Anyway, I'd deeped what the problem was and finally went to see my doctor when I couldn't get out of bed. This was on a day when there was a concert going on close to the hotel so it was booked out and I had to call in sick. Actually, lemme not lie, Ruby made me call my GP and call in sick. I told them what was going on. Not everything but most of it. And they said go A&E. They did a few tests now and apparently man had some gallbladder issues. I'm not even gonna lie, I didn't know what that was. But they said I needed to have an operation ASAP. Like I said, around these times, everything was hazy, so I don't really know how long I waited for the operation. But I know I told Kofi and he had my back about it. Said it was a minor, bare people have gallstones. Probably weren't drinking enough water.

Man, I missed Temi a lot, I remember that. She was so good to me. And I was coming up to the hardest part of my diet with no one there to have my back the way she did. The way we met, the timing was perfect. Some double journey starting at the same time. But I guess that's just the nature of life. You start something together and finish it alone. I had the operation. It only took about forty-five minutes apparently, but the doctors tried to keep me in hospital longer than they said. It was like they wanted to kidnap man. Once they moved me to a place where I could recover for the night, I swear they had one security guard at the end of my bed. Sometimes I'd catch him watching me. But yeah, I thought *fuck all that* and left. They wanted me to wait for a psychologist but I said no. Psychologist for what? Lemme go home, man.

Chapter 9

90lbs

Kofi knew what time I'd be leaving the hospital. I couldn't really walk properly, even though that tight feeling in my stomach was gone. I sat outside the hospital for ages. I think this was the first time I ever felt to cry without someone having caused it. I was so tired. A car started beeping its horn. It had been in the car park since I'd been sitting there. I know because it was the same whip Ruby had. I couldn't see the plates from where I was sitting, but after a while the beeping stopped and the car doors opened. Ruby, Omar and Werda stepped out, walked up to me and helped me into the car.

Chapter 10

85lbs

I was signed off from work as sick. Ruby said I could take as long as I wanted with full pay for up to six months. I was throwing up a lot of my food these times. I was having mad cravings too, but when I got whatever it was I wanted, I'd feel this mad fear going through my whole body. Sometimes I'd quickly put it in my mouth, chew it and then spit it out like I'd done before. But even the juice of whatever it was made me want to be sick. I couldn't even run. Or do crunches. Or do any weights. I swear. I'd do ten bodyweight squats and feel like I needed to sleep for like an hour. I didn't have anyone to do my body fat percentage as well. Kofi had basically ghosted me. He kept being like, *yeah, I'll shout you in a bit* whenever I messaged him. But I didn't hear from that guy. Same as

Ross. Focusing on their own training because I couldn't keep up anymore. That's fair enough, though. I couldn't even be mad at it. Everyone has their own stuff going on, get me. I couldn't become the distraction.

Chapter 11

80lbs

I never thought it would be painful just to walk. It wasn't even the tiredness. I could actually feel the bones in my feet when I was walking so I had to be bare careful. Man was tiptoeing everywhere. When I got to my GP for my checkup, though, he started talking about shit that had nothing to do with my gallbladder. Nothing to do with him, even. I don't know why everyone was so concerned with what I was trying to achieve. Like, aside from feeling hungry and in pain all the time, it was as if I was always holding back tears. People wouldn't leave me alone. And I knew something was going to cause me to break at some point. Most mornings I didn't even look at my phone. But anyway, I listened to what my doctor was saying. Said *yeah, I hear you* or just nodded my head. I remember thinking about being under a heavy weight. That moment where you think it's gonna drop on your face. But somehow, you pull out some next strength and get it up, control it down. I had none of that left in me. I think I failed while I was sitting there listening to my GP. I just agreed to whatever he was saying. And you know what, I actually cried. I cried so much that day. So much that I gave myself the maddest headache where if I shook my head, I could feel my brain moving about. I swear, it was mad. I still don't agree with the few things my doctor was saying. I don't think there's anything seriously wrong with me. But I can't lie, being shook to eat was actually making me shook full stop. Obviously I didn't wanna die. That's the whole reason I stopped eating ultra-processed food. This was just supposed to be about self-control. Reaching a goal. Being pure muscle, no soft bits, no fat. But the fear was a next ting. And I didn't want my mum to clock what was going on, either. So I just agreed to go. And I sat in my GP's office until an ambulance came and picked me up.

Chapter 12

So I think that's it, really. I think that's everything. From when I met Temi, to me being up in here. They don't force me to eat like I know they do with other people. One girl starts banging her head on the wall when she knows it's time to munch. Never thought I'd be in a place like this. But it is what it is. And Ruby comes to see me. But honestly, sometimes I'm physically shaking after everything I swallow. I do slip up sometimes and throw it up after a while. I asked one nurse to lock the toilet doors but she was saying they're not allowed. Honestly, I don't get how that helps, might as well feed us all with the tube. But it's whatever, I guess. I just try to think of Marcus Aurelius or Schopenhauer and suffering. It's life and I'll get through it. I know I will. Even though I don't feel better. Like, after expressing all this, I mean. I feel exactly the same. But maybe it takes time. And patience is my thing. Patience and discipline. I just wish I could see how much body fat I have. My stomach is always bloated but I know that's a lie. That don't mean I'm fat. I know it's a lie and I keep telling myself that. I'm not fat. I'm just bloated. But anyway, I'll keep getting this stuff out. My memory is still shit but day by day it's not so bad. I'll make it through this, trust me. Once they let me go home, I'll be back on my ting. The muscle is gonna look crazy.

Afterword

Ray passed away suddenly from complications due to anorexia nervosa. This is his short memoir, a slice of life from a difficult time, though he wasn't always aware of what he was going through. As the editor and co-author, I've taken a few liberties with both parts of the book, but tried to remain true to Ray's original voice and structure. Toward the latter part of the book, Ray's declining enthusiasm for documenting his experiences is clear, and I wanted to preserve that realism, regardless of how fractured it made the narrative. I used some of my own notes of the time to help flesh out a few of the missed details, the feelings I know Ray felt but was unable to articulate. It was challenging trying to stay true to his voice and perspective, especially during more problematic moments, but I hope the reader is able to see who he truly was. I know Ray wouldn't have wanted me to publish this, but I felt and still feel so strongly that his experiences can help others struggling the way he did. And I hope that adding my voice to his means that something new has been created. Something he could see as distinct enough not to be a violation of his trust and wishes. Ray was dedicated to recovery and I choose to believe he would have pushed through and been able to enjoy life again. With or without me. We weren't together through many of the events described, but I was present for most of his journey. Ray chose to omit me from the later part of his struggles. I'm not sure why and it does me no good to speculate, but I was there. Supportive and hopeful. I spoke to him every day and was with Ruby, Omar and Werda when we picked him up from the hospital. I also sat with him in his GP's office, holding his hand until the ambulance arrived. He was never alone. I hope he knew that. Ray will live on through his voice. Through his experiences. Through this book. And my love will finally have somewhere to go.

Temi Olurounbi

About Quick Reads

"Reading is such an important building block for success"

– Jojo Moyes

Quick Reads are short books written by bestselling authors.

Did you enjoy this Quick Read?

Tell us what you thought by filling in our short survey. Scan the QR code to go directly to the survey or visit:
bit.ly/QuickReads2026

Thank you to Penguin Random House, Hachette and all our publishing partners for their ongoing support.

A big thank you to Curtis Brown for supporting the 20th anniversary of Quick Reads.

A special thank you to Jojo Moyes for her generous donation in 2020–2022 which helped to build the future of Quick Reads.

Quick Reads is delivered by The Reading Agency, a UK charity that inspires social and personal change through the proven power of reading.

readingagency.org.uk @readingagency #QuickReads

The Reading Agency, Registered number: 3904882 (England & Wales)
Registered charity number: 1085443 (England & Wales)
Registered Office: 24 Bedford Row, London, WC1R 4EH
The Reading Agency is supported using public funding by
Arts Council England.

Find your next Quick Read

For 2026 we have 6 Quick Reads for you to enjoy:

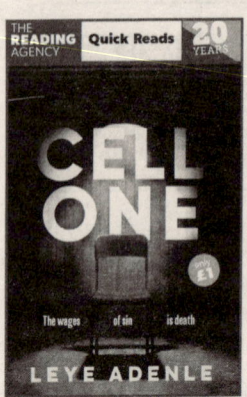

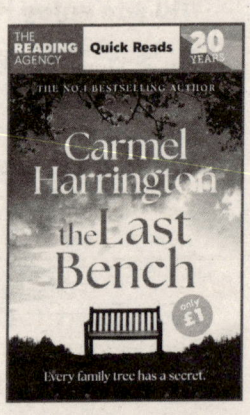

Quick Reads are available to buy in paperback or ebook and to borrow from your local library. For a complete list of titles and more information on the authors and their books visit: **readingagency.org.uk/quickreads**

Continue your reading journey with The Reading Agency:

Reading Ahead

Challenge yourself to complete six reads by taking part in **Reading Ahead** at your local library, college or workplace: **readingahead.org.uk**

Book Club Hub

Join the **Book Club Hub** to find a book club and discover new recommendations: **bookclubhub.co.uk**

World Book Night

Celebrate reading on **World Book Night,** every year on 23 April: **worldbooknight.org.uk**

Summer Reading Challenge

Read with your family as part of the **Summer Reading Challenge**: **summerreadingchallenge.org.uk**

For more information on our work and the power of reading visit: **readingagency.org.uk**

More from Quick Reads

If you enjoyed the 2026 Quick Reads, please explore our 6 titles from 2025:

For a complete list of titles and more information on the authors and their books visit: **readingagency.org.uk/quickreads**

PENGUIN BOOKS

UK | USA | Canada | Ireland | Australia
India | New Zealand | South Africa

Penguin Books is part of the Penguin Random House group of companies
whose addresses can be found at global.penguinrandomhouse.com

Penguin Random House UK,
One Embassy Gardens, 8 Viaduct Gardens, London SW11 7BW

penguin.co.uk

First published 2026
003

Copyright © Derek Owusu, 2026

The moral right of the author has been asserted

This is a work of fiction. Unless otherwise indicated, all the names, characters, businesses, places, events and incidents in this book are either the product of the author's imagination or used in a fictitious manner. Any resemblance to actual persons, living or dead, or actual events is purely coincidental.

Penguin Random House values and supports copyright. Copyright fuels creativity, encourages diverse voices, promotes freedom of expression and supports a vibrant culture. Thank you for purchasing an authorised edition of this book and for respecting intellectual property laws by not reproducing, scanning or distributing any part of it by any means without permission. You are supporting authors and enabling Penguin Random House to continue to publish books for everyone. No part of this book may be used or reproduced in any manner for the purpose of training artificial intelligence technologies or systems. In accordance with Article 4(3) of the DSM Directive 2019/790, Penguin Random House expressly reserves this work from the text and data mining exception.

Set in 12/16pt Stone Serif ITC Pro
Typeset by Six Red Marbles UK, Thetford, Norfolk

Printed and bound in Great Britain by Clays Ltd, Elcograf S.p.A.

The authorised representative in the EEA is Penguin Random House Ireland,
Morrison Chambers, 32 Nassau Street, Dublin D02 YH68

A CIP catalogue record for this book is available from the British Library

ISBN: 978-1-804-96308-1

Penguin Random House is committed to a sustainable future
for our business, our readers and our planet. This book is made
from Forest Stewardship Council® certified paper.